ROSIE the TRUFFLE HOUND

jessie hartland

◉ NANCY PAULSEN BOOKS

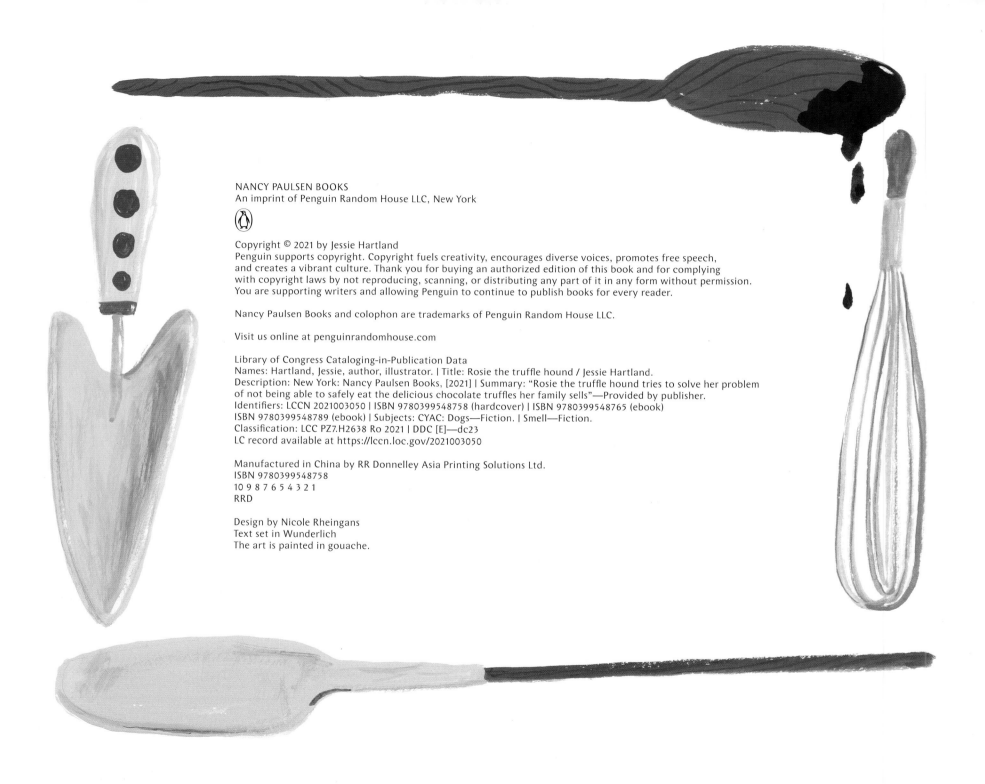

NANCY PAULSEN BOOKS
An imprint of Penguin Random House LLC, New York

Nancy Paulsen Books and colophon are trademarks of Penguin Random House LLC.

Visit us online at penguinrandomhouse.com

Library of Congress Cataloging-in-Publication Data
Names: Hartland, Jessie, author, illustrator. | Title: Rosie the truffle hound / Jessie Hartland.
Description: New York: Nancy Paulsen Books, [2021] | Summary: "Rosie the truffle hound tries to solve her problem
of not being able to safely eat the delicious chocolate truffles her family sells"—Provided by publisher.
Identifiers: LCCN 2021003050 | ISBN 9780399548758 (hardcover) | ISBN 9780399548765 (ebook)
ISBN 9780399548789 (ebook) | Subjects: CYAC: Dogs—Fiction. | Smell—Fiction.
Classification: LCC PZ7.H2638 Ro 2021 | DDC [E]—dc23
LC record available at https://lccn.loc.gov/2021003050

Manufactured in China by RR Donnelley Asia Printing Solutions Ltd.
ISBN 9780399548758
10 9 8 7 6 5 4 3 2 1
RRD

Design by Nicole Rheingans
Text set in Wunderlich
The art is painted in gouache.

for Carl,

and in the memory

of our two poodles,

Clementine + Django

ROSIE is a dog with a keen sense of smell. She knows when a pie is coming out of an oven three houses over. She can smell a sizzling frank on a grill a mile away.

She can even smell the stale breath of a snoring mole deep in the woods.

Rosie lives in a cozy house
down a winding path,
set in the middle
of a forest of
towering trees.

It's nice, but she
has nothing to do.

The other dogs mostly sleep all day, chase squirrels, or watch TV.

Rosie prefers to sit outside
and smell the roses.

Her family loves her, but they are always busy
making chocolate truffles to sell in their shop.
The chocolate truffles smell *so good*.

But Rosie can't eat them because,
as you may know,
chocolate is poisonous for dogs.

Poor Rosie!

So one day,
she runs away.

Rosie's family is sad.
They put signs up everywhere,
but Rosie is far away.

Where is Rosie?

She's in the big city, smelling the big-city smells: pizza baking, garbage stewing, and scrumptious street food.

But there's no time for sightseeing!

Rosie needs a job.

She is lucky to get a job as
a guard dog in a museum.
But the job is so boring,
she falls asleep.

She gets fired.

She tries being
a show dog.
It is glamorous,
but Rosie does
not like fussing
with her hair.

And the smells
are dreadful!

When she gets a job as a guide dog, her nose gets her in trouble.

Then one day, she gets a whiff of a different sort of job.

The next morning, she bikes out beyond the city
to a cool, pungent forest of oak and hazelnut trees.

A man greets Rosie.

These truffles are not the chocolate kind!
They are fungi—like mushrooms—
and they grow underground near the roots
of old nut trees. They are *not* so easy to find.
That's where the good nose comes in.

Truffles, being so tricky to find, are *very* expensive.

Fortunately, they are quite flavorful,
so just a little bit is enough.

Chefs love to cook with truffles.

black truffle risotto

scrambled eggs 'n' truffles

tagliatelle al tartufo

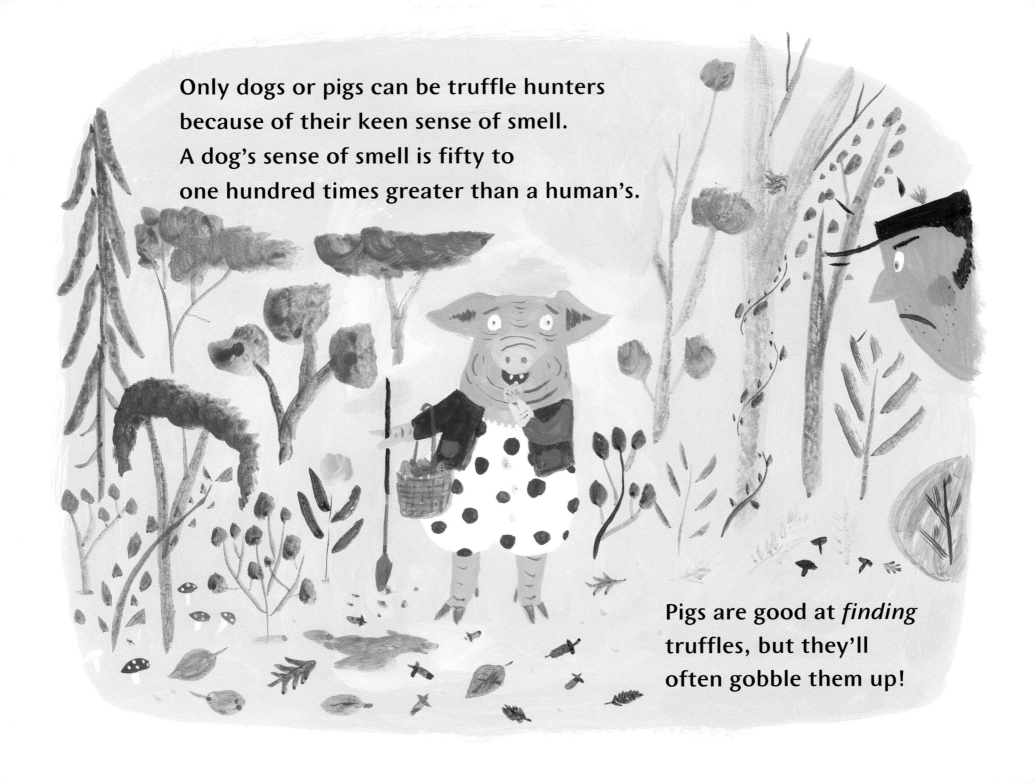

Only dogs or pigs can be truffle hunters
because of their keen sense of smell.
A dog's sense of smell is fifty to
one hundred times greater than a human's.

Pigs are good at *finding*
truffles, but they'll
often gobble them up!

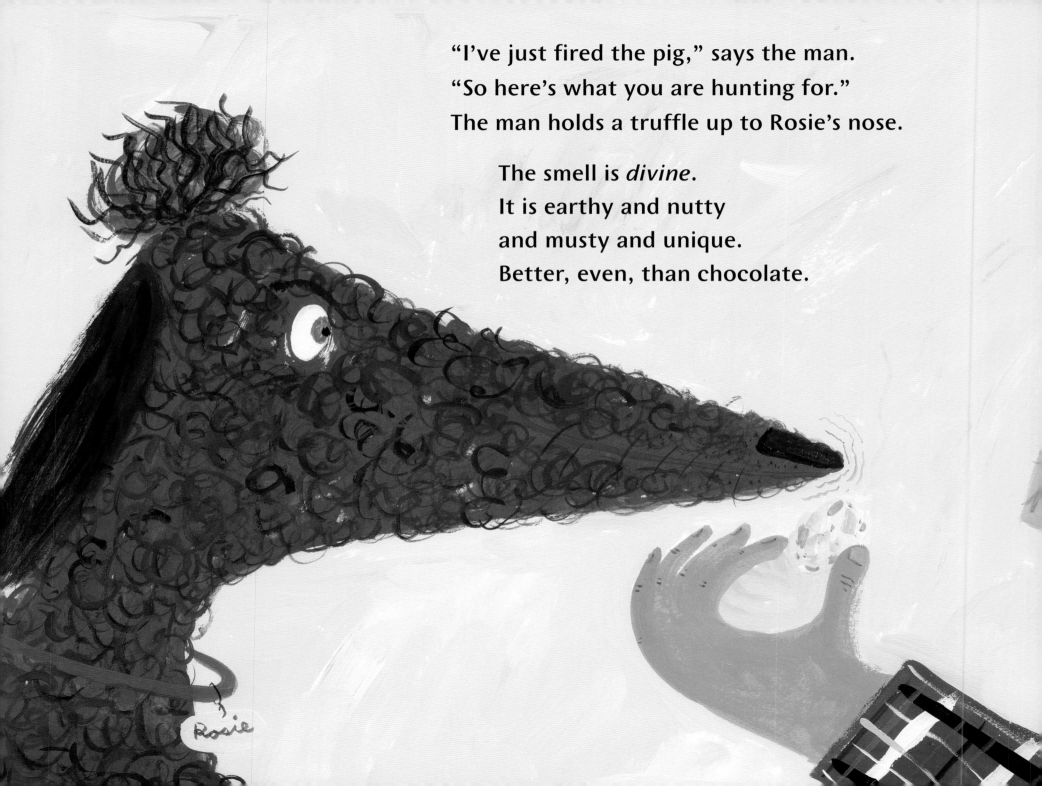

"I've just fired the pig," says the man.
"So here's what you are hunting for."
The man holds a truffle up to Rosie's nose.

The smell is *divine*.
It is earthy and nutty
and musty and unique.
Better, even, than chocolate.

"When you get a whiff of one of these,
dig, baby, dig. But *carefully*!

And then
put the truffle
in this basket."

At first, Rosie digs up an old shoe!

But soon she is very good at her new job.
Her boss is very happy with her work.

At the end of the week,
she has a brand-new bicycle.

But Rosie is sad. Digging up truffles in the woods is a lonely job. She longs to be with her family.

So one day, she rides back to the house
set in the middle of a forest of towering trees.

"Do I smell what I think I smell?" says Rosie as she rides down the winding path.

She takes a close sniff of the ground, digs a bit, and YES! She recognizes that *divine* smell . . .

TRUFFLES!

Rosie's family can't believe their eyes.

And they can't believe their ears when they hear what's growing in their woods.

Now the shop sells *both* kinds of truffles—
the chocolate ones and the fungi ones.

Rosie is happy. She spends her days digging truffles
and working in the shop. She is surrounded by her family
and the delicious smell of truffles—both kinds.

Bon appétit!

ROSIE'S chocolate truffles

Ask a grown-up to help you with boiling liquid on the stove!

Ingredients:
- 8 ounces good-quality semisweet chocolate, chopped fine
- 1/2 cup heavy cream
- 2 teaspoons vanilla extract
- 1/2 cup unsweetened cocoa powder

1. Put chopped chocolate in a small heat-proof bowl. Bring cream to a boil in a small saucepan, then pour it over the chocolate and let it sit for 5 minutes. Stir until it is smooth, then add vanilla. Refrigerate for at least 3 hours. Then scoop up small spoonfuls and shape them into 1-inch balls.
2. Put cocoa powder into another small bowl. Roll the chocolate balls in the cocoa. Your hands will soon be a mess!
3. Refrigerate until firm.
4. Store in refrigerator for up to 2 weeks.

Rosie's Noodles with truffles

Ask a grown-up to help you with boiling liquid on the stove!

Ingredients:
- 1/3 pound dried pasta
- 5 tablespoons unsalted butter
- 1 small truffle, black or white

1. Cook the noodles according to box directions. Reserve 1/4 cup of the pasta water.
2. Melt the butter in a medium-size saucepan over low heat. Add the cooked pasta and pasta water; stir for a minute. Remove from heat and pour pasta into a serving bowl.
3. Grate the truffle on top and stir for 2 minutes. Add salt and pepper to taste.

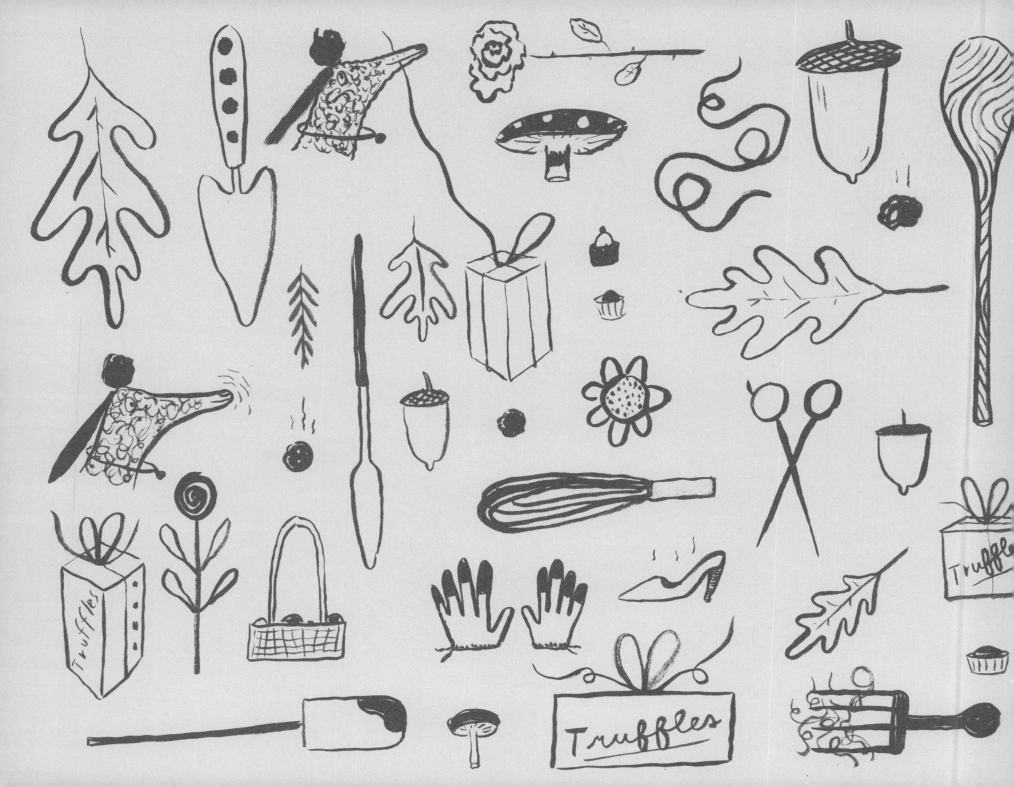